Agnes
and the
Giant

by Anne Adeney and Daniel Postgate

W
FRANKLIN WATTS
LONDON•SYDNEY

First published in 2009 by
Franklin Watts
338 Euston Road
London
NW1 3BH

Franklin Watts Australia
Level 17/207 Kent Street
Sydney
NSW 2000

Text © Anne Adeney 2009
Illustrations © Daniel Postgate 2009

The rights of Anne Adeney to be identified as the author
and Daniel Postgate as the illustrator of this Work have been asserted
in accordance with the Copyright, Designs and Patents Act, 1988.

A CIP catalogue record for this book is available
from the British Library.

ISBN 978 0 7496 8552 2 (hbk)
ISBN 978 0 7496 8564 5 (pbk)

Series Editor: Jackie Hamley
Series Advisor: Dr Barrie Wade
Series Designer: Peter Scoulding

Printed in China

Franklin Watts is a division of
Hachette Children's Books,
an Hachette UK company
www.hachette.co.uk

Long ago, the land of Cornwall
was still full of huge giants.

On the rocky northern coast lived a giant called Bolster. He was so big that he could stand with his feet on different hills.

The villagers were terrified of
Bolster. The enormous giant ate
sheep for breakfast, cows for
dinner and *people* for supper.

Everyone ran to the caves whenever they heard Bolster coming along.

The ground shook as Bolster
thundered towards their village.

People grabbed their children and
hid. Bolster's favourite snack was
a couple of juicy children.

The villagers sent messengers throughout the kingdom, begging for help. Many brave knights came and tried to kill the giant ...

... but Bolster could not be beaten. "I can beat **anyone** and do **anything**!" he boasted.

A young girl called Agnes lived
in the village. She was kind and
gentle and she hated the evil
giant. Agnes was also very
clever and she had a plan.

Agnes decided to challenge Bolster herself. She bravely climbed up to the giant's lair and called out to him.

"Where's Bolster, the cowardly
giant?" she shouted. "I hear even
a sheep is cleverer than him."

Bolster roared with rage.
"I can beat **anyone**
and do **anything**!"

"Prove it!" said Agnes. "I'll give you a task so you can prove your boast."

"I'll prove it!" yelled Bolster. "Then I'll eat you!"

Agnes showed Bolster a small pool on the cliff top. "Fill this pool with your blood to prove that you can do anything," she said.

Bolster cackled with joy. Filling such a tiny pool would be easy for him. He cut his hand.

"The blood from just one of my fingers will fill this pool!" he boasted.

But Agnes knew better. The pool was joined to the sea by a long crack in the rocks.

Bolster's blood poured into the
pool – and out of it – like water
running down a plughole.

The giant got weaker and weaker
as his blood drained away through
the rock and into the sea.

25

At last, Bolster toppled and rolled over the edge of the cliff.

He went crashing down into the
angry sea, never to be seen again!

Hundreds of years later, Agnes became a saint and the Cornish town still bears her name
– St Agnes.

And you can still see the red stain
on the cliffs, where Bolster's
blood drained away.

Puzzle 1

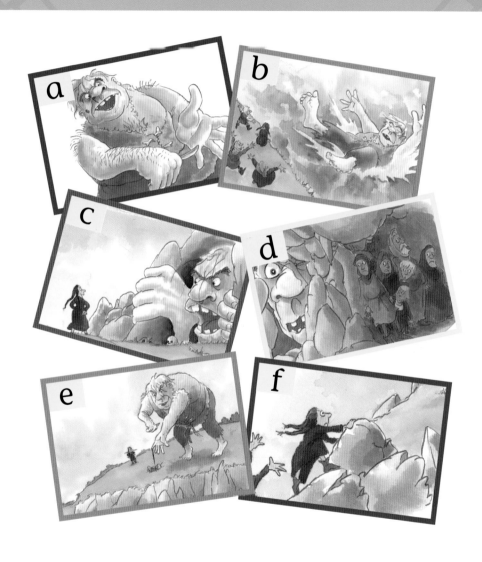

Put these pictures in the correct order.
Which event do you think is most important?
Now try writing the story in your own words!

Puzzle 2

1. Will he find us in here?

2. I'm bigger and stronger than everyone!

3. No one can beat me!

4. Don't let him eat the children!

5. Can you prove your boast?

6. You're just a stupid giant!

Choose the correct speech bubbles for each character. Can you think of any others? Turn over to find the answers.

Answers

Puzzle 1

The correct order is: 1d, 2f, 3c, 4a, 5e, 6b

Puzzle 2

Agnes: 5, 6

Bolster: 2, 3

Villagers: 1, 4

Look out for more Hopscotch Adventures:

Aladdin and the **Lamp**
ISBN 978 0 7496 6692 7

Blackbeard the **Pirate**
ISBN 978 0 7496 6690 3

George and the **Dragon**
ISBN 978 0 7496 6691 0

Jack the **Giant-Killer**
ISBN 978 0 7496 6693 4

Beowulf and **Grendel**
ISBN 978 0 7496 8551 5*
*ISBN 978 0 7496 8563 8

Agnes and the **Giant**
ISBN 978 0 7496 8552 2*
ISBN 978 0 7496 8564 5

The Dragon and the **Pudding**
ISBN 978 0 7496 8549 2*
ISBN 978 0 7496 8561 4

Finn MacCool and the **Giant's Causeway**
ISBN 978 0 7496 8550 8*
ISBN 978 0 7496 8562 1

TALES OF KING ARTHUR

1. **The Sword in the Stone**
ISBN 978 0 7496 6694 1

2. **Arthur the King**
ISBN 978 0 7496 6695 8

3. **The Round Table**
ISBN 978 0 7496 6697 2

4. **Sir Lancelot** and the **Ice Castle**
ISBN 978 0 7496 6698 9

5. **Sir Gawain** and the **Green Knight**
ISBN 978 0 7496 8557 7*
ISBN 978 0 7496 8569 0

6. **Sir Galahad** and the **Holy Grail**
ISBN 978 0 7496 8558 4*
ISBN 978 0 7496 8570 6

TALES OF ROBIN HOOD

Robin and the **Knight**
ISBN 978 0 7496 6699 6

Robin and the **Monk**
ISBN 978 0 7496 6700 9

Robin and the **Silver Arrow**
ISBN 978 0 7496 6703 0

Robin and the **Friar**
ISBN 978 0 7496 6702 3

Robin and the **Butcher**
ISBN 978 0 7496 8555 3*
ISBN 978 0 7496 8568 3

Robin and **Maid Marian**
ISBN 978 0 7496 8556 0*
ISBN 978 0 7496 8567 6

For more Hopscotch books go to:
www.franklinwatts.co.uk

* hardback   **Tales of Sinbad the Sailor also available!**